Hooray! It's a New Royal Baby!

by Martha Mumford   illustrated by Ada Grey

BLOOMSBURY
LONDON   NEW DELHI   NEW YORK   SYDNEY

The Royal Palace was bustling with excitement.
The Duke and Duchess were bringing home the
New Royal Baby.

Please return / renew by date shown.
You can renew it at:
norlink.norfolk.gov.uk
or by telephone: 0344 800 8006
Please have your library card & PIN ready

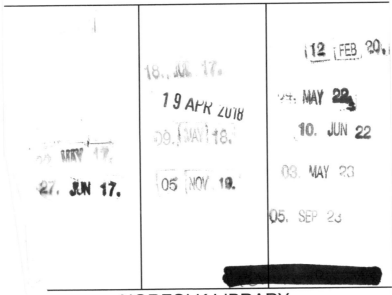

18.. JUL 17.

19 APR 2018

09. MAY 18.

05 NOV 19.

MAY 17.

27. JUN 17.

12 FEB 20.

24. MAY 22

10. JUN 22

03. MAY 23

05. SEP 23

NORFOLK LIBRARY
AND INFORMATION SERVICE

In the nursery, the royal rocking horse was being polished, the rabbit mobile was being hung above the royal crib and the teddy bears were neatly placed in rows.

Meanwhile, at the palace gates, Royal Baby George was helping his auntie and uncle to hang welcome bunting and new baby balloons.

"Just think,"
said his auntie,
"you are going to have a
tiny New Royal Baby to
make friends with.
It will be such fun!"

RAY! IT'S A NEW ROYAL BABY!

But Royal Baby George wasn't sure.
What if the New Royal Baby wanted
to play with all his toys?

What if the New Royal Baby
tried to snatch his jam sandwiches?

Worse still, what if the New Royal Baby
dribbled over his favourite toy dinosaur?

In fact, the more Royal Baby
George thought about it, the
more he didn't want a New
Royal Baby – AT ALL!

As the royal car pulled up outside the palace, everybody cheered. But Royal Baby George just looked glum.

The Duchess gave him a hug.

"Come and see our new baby,"
she whispered softly.
"You are a very important big brother now.
My very special big boy."

Royal Baby George thought the New Royal Baby's face was scrunched up and wrinkly.

Waaah!

Waaah!

Waaah!

The New Royal Baby started to cry.

Then . . .

Waaah!

Waaah!

Waaah!

Royal Baby George started to cry, too.
"Oh dear," said the Duke.
"You really are like two peas in a pod."
The Duchess picked up Royal Baby George
and gave him a hug, "Come on, let's go inside."

Everyone wanted to catch a glimpse
of the new arrival.

"Ooh, what a beautiful
bouncing baby,"
cooed the cook.

"Such cute rosy
cheeks," gushed
the gardener.

"A real sweetie,"
squeaked the baby's auntie.

"A corker,"
agreed the baby's uncle.

Royal Baby George stepped
across to take another look –
the New Royal Baby didn't
seem to be doing a great deal
of bouncing.

In fact, the New Royal
Baby didn't seem to be
doing very much at
all – except for making
sucking noises.

Royal Baby George thought the New Royal
Baby looked more like a goldfish than a baby.
"No want baby," he said.
"Want fishy."

And that gave the
Duke an idea . . .

Later that day, when Royal Baby George was happily playing dinosaurs, the Duke whispered, "Come and see — the New Royal Baby has got you a special present to say thank you for being a big brother."

Royal Baby George couldn't believe his eyes. His very own goldfish!

Perhaps the New Royal Baby wasn't so bad after all. He tiptoed over to the crib and gave the little one a gentle kiss.

Royal Baby George loved his new goldfish.
He watched it swim round and round the bowl,
under the bridge, through the plants. Then he
watched it swim round again . . . and again.

The goldfish seemed to like doing the
same thing — ALL the time.
It was getting a bit boring.

But, as for the New Royal Baby, well that was
a different matter altogether. The New Royal
Baby was learning new things all the time . . .

like smiling at
Royal Baby George,

gurgling,

rolling over,

crawling like a caterpillar

and blowing raspberries!

Every day was different with the New
Royal Baby around. Royal Baby George loved
tickling the baby's tummy and hearing the giggles.

He loved bouncing the bouncy
chair and making the baby giggle
even more.

And he especially loved making a mess
with the New Royal Baby at mealtimes.

Things became a bit trickier when the
New Royal Baby got some teeth.

And when the New Royal
Baby started to take a fancy
to Royal Baby George's toys.

Bathtimes could sometimes get
a bit TOO wet.

EEEK!

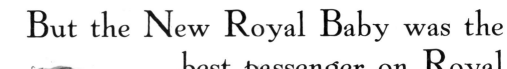

But the New Royal Baby was the best passenger on Royal Baby George's bus,

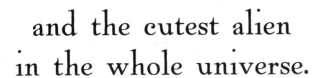

the funniest pirate on his pirate ship,

and the cutest alien in the whole universe.

On the whole, Royal Baby George decided that having a New Royal Baby was much more fun than having a new goldfish.

"Maybe it's time for another one?" smiled the Duke.

But, that night, as everyone snored away . . .

Waaah!
Waaah!
Waaah!

"Maybe not just yet," sighed a weary Duchess.

For the marvellous Fiz and the wonderful Kristina — MM

For Vicki, Emma, Fiz and Kristina — AG

Bloomsbury Publishing, London, New Delhi, New York and Sydney

First published in Great Britain in 2015 by Bloomsbury Publishing Plc
50 Bedford Square, London, WC1B 3DP

A CIP catalogue record for this book is available from the British Library

ISBN 978 1 4088 6571 2 (PB)

ISBN 978 1 4088 6570 5 (ebook)

Printed in Italy by L.E.G.O Spa

1 3 5 7 9 10 8 6 4 2

All papers used by Bloomsbury Publishing are natural, recyclable products made
from wood grown in well managed forests. The manufacturing processes conform
to the environmental regulations of the country of origin

www.bloomsbury.com